Max's
Wild Night

Books by Meg Welch Dendler

<u>Cats in the Mirror</u> Series

Book 1: *Why Kimba Saved The World*
Book 2: *Vacation Hiro*
Book 3: *Miss Fatty Cat's Revenge*
Book 4: *Slinky Steps Out*

And the Companion Books
Max's Wild Night
Dottie's Daring Day

Also by Meg Welch Dendler
At the Corner of Magnetic and Main

Max's Wild Night

by
Meg Welch Dendler

SERENITY MOUNTAIN PUBLISHING
Eureka Springs, Arkansas

Published by Serenity Mountain Publishing

Max's Wild Night
©2015 by Meg Welch Dendler. All rights reserved.
Printed in the United States of America.

www.megdendler.com

First Edition, Second Printing

ISBN - 13: 978-1508606734
ISBN - 10: 1508606730

Cover design by Lesley Hollinger Vernon at
www.lvdesignhouse.com.
Drawings by Callista Rose Dendler.
Photos by Scott and Meg Dendler.
Chapter icon of Max by Scott Dendler.

Dedication:

Happy 10th Birthday, Max!

Thank you for putting up with us and all
of your cats for the last eight years,
and many more to come.

Max, about two years old

Even if I'm left high and dry at the end of this wild journey, just taking it is a great feeling.

Olivia Wilde

WILD AND FREE

Max didn't mean to run away. Well, not exactly. Not at first.

The day had started out badly, and then it got worse. When the Daddy-man let Max out of the nighttime kennel and then outside for breakfast, the man became distracted and forgot playtime. Their morning routine was for Max to check out every inch of his Ozark mountaintop yard, snuffling around for each and every new scent. As long as he stayed out of the woods, the Daddy-man let him explore as much as he liked. Then they might have a quick game of chase or check on the vegetables in the garden. It was a special outdoor time together each day. But not this morning.

Max heard the man talking to one of the daughters about a science project, and there was lots of scurrying around and loading strange looking cardboard things into the car. The Daddy-man drove away with Leia and didn't even say goodbye. Max was left with the Mama-lady. Morning was not a playtime for her.

"Come on inside, Max. Let's go. What are you waiting for?" she said, not understanding the routine.

I'm waiting for playtime, he thought.

Max had lived long enough to know that Mama was not a morning-loving person, and she was not going to come outside and play. He plodded back into the house, head hung low. There would be no playtime this morning.

But that wasn't the worst of it. Max just kept getting into trouble, even though he didn't mean to.

If that little white cat kept running by his special pillow spot, Max couldn't resist nipping at her tail at least once. What dog could? The cat was teasing him, but the Mama-lady always took her side.

"Max, did you just try to bite her? Bad Dog!"

Bad Dog. The worst words in the whole English language. This might have been the first, but it wasn't the last time a human would say them to Max that day.

Max got bored and wandered into the cat's special area to sneak a nibble or two of food. *Bad Dog.*

He found something like one of his bones to chew on. It was white and leathery and felt good under his teeth. *Gnaw. Gnaw.* But it was not a bone. It was a shoe. *Bad Dog.*

A delivery man drove up in a big brown truck, and Max barked and barked to let him know that this house was not to be messed with. *Woof! Woof! Woof!* Cats scattered and hid under beds. Mama wandered over to the door, waving the dog away and telling him to hush.

"Max, it's just the UPS man. You see him all the time. Shush! Goodness!"

Max did not shush until he had scared the man all the way down the long driveway and kept his house safe. The Mama-lady was not impressed. *Bad Dog*.

After his morning nap, Max hoped things would get better. He tried to be good, but keeping track of the Mama-lady was his number one job in the world. Especially when the man was gone. And she wouldn't be still or stay in one place. She tripped on him coming out of the kitchen. She bumped into him when she went into the bedroom. And again when she came out.

Finally, when she was heading to the laundry room with an overloaded basket, Max helped her along by directing her steps with his awesome herding, side-to-side jumps. The Mama-lady had had enough.

"Max, stop it. I can get to the laundry room on my own. Go-lie-down-Max."

Okay. It wasn't a *Bad Dog*, but it felt like one. Max slunk over to his pillow and stayed there until dinner time. Even that most special time of the day— dinner—the event Max waited for all afternoon, was bad.

The Daddy-man did all the same things he normally does. Max saw him get the spoon from the drawer and head to the magic cabinet that held the cans of meaty goodness, but the man was annoyed by Max's routine dinner-dance. Leaping around by the back door, Max accidentally trampled all over the shoes that had been left there. He didn't mean to. They were just in the way.

"Max, get off the shoes!" the Daddy-man said.

Max had hoped for some extra after-dinner playtime, but it was cut short instead. The Daddy-man was distracted by other things and didn't pay much attention to Max. The dog slunk back into the house and plopped down on his pillow.

He pouted the rest of the evening, but no one seemed to notice. His humans were all busy with their own things and didn't even look his way. At least no one was angry with him. With a deep sigh, Max curled up tight and wondered what life would be like without all of these people always bossing him around, being so grumpy, and taking him for granted.

When the Daddy-man let him out to go potty before bedtime, Max discovered the most amazing smell by a tree at the far end of the yard. The day was going to end well, after all! Chasing a great smell around the yard was one of Max's favorite activities. Nose to the rocky earth and tail wagging rhythmically up high in the air, Max snuffled along the dark ground in a path that led him farther and farther away from the house.

Even when the Ozark Mountain ground became steep and rocky under his feet, and he slid as much as he actually walked, Max followed the trail. When the tall trees became thicker and thicker, Max still followed the trail. He could hear the Daddy-man calling his name more and more urgently, but it didn't matter. He was focused on the trail. It is impossible to drop concentration for even a moment when you're lured by the invisible trail of a magnificent odor in the woods after dark. Every dog knows that. He couldn't break his concentration. He would never find the trail again.

By the time Max raised his head from the ground, he didn't recognize anything around him. The trail had gone cold, and search as he might, he couldn't figure where it went from there. The remarkable animal was lost forever, never to be traced again. Now he stood in the silent, moonlit woods, all alone.

Far away in the distance, Max heard the Daddy-man

calling his name. It echoed off the nearby mountains and flowed through the valley.

"Max! Come on, Max!" A trill of the Daddy-man's whistle, the one that meant *come now*, reached his ears.

Sniffing the fresh spring air, Max couldn't locate his house or his yard, and he couldn't tell exactly what direction the calls were coming from. In the Good Dog part of his mind, Max knew that if he just turned directly around and started climbing up, he would probably get back home again. Home was up at the top somewhere.

But as he pondered this, an owl hooted above his head and then flew away into the night. Max jumped into a defensive position, his feet wide apart, the hackles on his back raised. But something else deep in his soul awakened—it was wild and had been passed down from his wolfy ancestors generations ago. It crept up from the rocky ground through his toes, up his legs, and tingled along his spine. Max realized he was free. Had he ever been this separate from humans before? Never.

Glancing up the mountain toward the house, Max

thought of the closed doors and the rules that governed every moment of his day.

Leave that cat alone, Max.

That's not your food, Max.

Stop drooling everywhere, Max.

Don't chew on that, Max.

Move. You're in the way, Max.

What's that smell? Oh, Max.

Go-Lie-Down-Max.

And the worst one of all. The one that made his heart ache every time: *Bad Dog, Max!*

The four cats slept on the furniture, climbed on the kitchen counters, and did whatever they jolly-well pleased. Max got yelled at if he even went into the kitchen. The Mama-lady said he was always underfoot and in the way in there. Just because the cats could slink in and out and were smaller didn't mean they had more right to be close to the Mama-lady than he did. He was in charge of the Mama-lady's safety and protection. He needed to keep an eye on her, but she was always shooing him away.

All of his Border Collie instincts told him that he was responsible for the lives of everyone in his house, but the humans and the cats only got annoyed with his attempts to direct and care for them.

"Quit trying to herd me, Max!" the Daddy-man said at least once a day.

The man couldn't understand that it was a dog's duty. It was his obligation. The cats were even less impressed and just hissed and swiped at his nose when he tried to convince them of the right direction to go. Even a blue-ribbon, champion herder could not be expected to organize cats. Max was sure of it.

On top of that, all of his Labrador instincts told him that he should be with the humans at all times as their companion, but the humans defied him at every turn. They were constantly leaving the house without him. The cats were allowed to sleep on the beds at night, but Max was locked in his crate in another room. The Mama-lady said something about naughty dogs who chew things up. All he knew was that he was being kept from his instinctive duties.

Standing there in the woods alone, the magnitude of the unfairness of his whole life churned through

Max. From the moment he was left at the animal shelter right after he was born, to the time the Mama-lady took him home a year later, until that very day, Max was a prisoner. But not now.

Now Max was free. He had the whole world in front of him. No one would tell him where he could and couldn't sit. Mama-lady wouldn't shut him in a crate tonight. No one would call him Bad Dog.

A light flashed past him, and the crunch of dried leaves and dead branches on the forest floor sounded from behind. Loose rocks rolled through the undergrowth, stirred up as the man worked his way down the mountain trying to find his dog in the dark.

"Max?" he heard the Daddy-man calling. "Max, get up here!" The whistle trilled again, louder this time.

Max had been almost-lost a couple of times before. Just like that night, he had followed a trail a short way into the woods at bedtime, and the Daddy-man had come after him with the flashlight and found him. The man had been really angry. Max remembered that much. *Bad Dog.* He was supposed to return to the man when he called and whistled. The wrestling of wild and tame instincts made his shoulder muscles twitch and his tail thrash.

All he had to do was stand still and be found. The flashlight beams and crunching noises were getting closer. The Daddy-man would find him soon. Or…

With a snort and a leap, Max turned and ran. The crunching of leaves and the jingling of the tags on his collar were the only evidence of his escape. He ran and ran until he came to the log fence that marked the edge of his property. Even on their longest walks, the Daddy-man never let him jump through the fence.

"No, Max," he would say. "That's not our land. The fence is as far as you go."

Tonight, there was nothing to stop him. Jumping between the wooden logs of the fence that surrounded their property, the black-and-white dog entered a forbidden domain. A full moon shone through the branches just enough to light his way. Splashing through a small stream, Max ran on without looking back.

Wild and free. He was totally and absolutely and undeniably wild and free.

Jumping between the wooden logs of the fence that surrounded their property, the black-and-white dog entered a forbidden domain.

THE VALLEY

Max ran until he burst from the woods into the valley at the bottom of the mountain. A full moon lit up the grassy field almost as brightly as the daylight, and the dog's eyes worked their magic to help him see almost as well as a cat at night.

Two brown cows lifted their heads and looked at him with sleepy eyes, their jaws working round and round on the grass of their last meal. Scattered over the rest of the field, he noticed other brown-and-white lumps, some standing and others crouched on the ground asleep. Plopping down at the edge of the tree line, Max panted and gasped for air. His heart pounded in his chest, the blood flowing so fast it made the tips of his ears tingle. He hadn't run that hard, maybe ever. It felt fantastic!

Catching his breath, the dog wasn't sure what came next. Every moment of his day was governed by someone else. He never got to make decisions about where to go and what to do. This newfound freedom was exhilarating.

The valley was full of amazing smells. Some of them came from the cows themselves and were not very interesting. There were Black Angus cows right across the highway from his house, and he had grown bored of their aromas long ago. Max made a quick survey of the ground around him for something more intriguing.

Skunk. He detected that one first. *Snerk.* A good sneeze cleared the smell from his sensitive nostrils. Max had learned all about skunks a few years ago. He could vividly remember that night. He'd picked up the trail of one of the stinky black-and-white animals when they lived in Texas. The Daddy-man and the two daughters, Mindy and Leia, had been out looking for a geocache in a park near the house. Little Leia had ahold of Max's leash, but once he caught that alluring scent, she was no match for him. Her cries for help brought the other two running as Max dragged her, bumping along behind him across the grass.

Mindy got there just in time to grab the leash as Max caught up to the skunk. Remembering the horror of that moment made the fur along his spine rise up and his eyes water. That tiny little creature looked like one of his cats at home, but none of his cats had ever pulled off a trick like that skunky monster. It flipped around, lifted its fluffy tail, and *pssstttsss pssstttsss* sprayed the most disgusting ick ever imaginable in the world all over the dog's face. Squeals from Mindy let him know that she was a victim too. Nasty. Nasty. Nasty.

At least no one had said *Bad Dog* to him that skunky night. The stench he could not run from or rub off in the grass, no matter how hard he tried, must have been punishment enough. When they got back to the house, it even looked like the Mama-lady was giving the Daddy-man the Bad Dog scolding for not stopping the skunk attack.

After two baths with the garden hose in a foul smelling, sudsy mess (at least it didn't smell as bad as the skunk ick), Max was allowed back into the house. The Mama-lady said he still smelled like a dead fish, but it would have to do. With no humans around to help him recover, Max had no intention of following that skunk trail tonight. He returned to his snuffling, in search of something more appealing.

When he hit an unfamiliar smell, Max knew that his next mission was clear. He would follow this trail wherever it led, and no one would stop him. Tail on full alert, swinging slowly from side to side, Max discovered which direction the scent was stronger. Nose to the ground, he trotted along, unaware of anything else around him. The bizarre noise that broke his concentration wasn't new, but he'd never heard it so close up and loud.

"Haaawww heeehaaaww heeehaaawww," the mule brayed.

Max froze in his tracks. Without lifting his nose from the ground, he eyed the creature up the field from him. The mule's ears were at full attention, and

Max saw the whites of his eyes and the gleam of bared teeth in the moonlight. The cows shuffled around in response to the mule's agitation.

"Get out of my field!" the mule hollered. Max was about to answer, but then he realized that the mule wasn't looking at him at all.

Canine laughter that made his spine tingle echoed through the valley, and Max lifted his nose. He forgot all about the trail. Fear crept into his bones and made his legs go weak when he saw who the mule was really yelling at.

3
COYOTES

J ust a few feet away from him, three shaggy coyotes stood their ground against the bared teeth of the mule. The dog had been so focused on the trail he was following that he had not smelled them right next to him.

Max had never met a coyote. Not face-to-face. When the weather got chilly and the Daddy-man made a campfire in the backyard for the family, the four humans would sit out long after dark at the top of their mountain. They would chat and gaze at the city lights far in the distance. On those special nights, the dog had heard his wild cousins yipping and howling in the valley. Others would answer from the valley on the other side of his mountain. They were always far away and talking about things he didn't really understand, so he never paid them much attention. Tonight, ignoring them was not an option.

The largest of the tawny wild dogs stepped toward the mule and lowered his head, a low, rumbling growl vibrating from his throat. His partners stood alertly behind him, ears perked and alert, and dark eyes glittering in the bright moonlight.

Max wasn't even sure if they had noticed him. Maybe his black fur had kept him hidden in the shadows of the trees. He lowered his head again so his speckled white neck fur and nose wouldn't give him away. Maybe the coyotes were too focused on the mule and his interference with their dinner plans to notice a house pet on the sidelines.

"Where do you have the calves tucked away on this lovely evening?" the alpha coyote snarled.

"As if I would tell you, you mangy killer."

The mule lowered his head, teeth still bared. Max

could see the mule's hind muscles twitching, ready to defend himself and the babies of his farmer's herd. Excitement and tension flowed through the air at a level that the dog had never felt before. Wild. It was all wonderfully and terrifyingly wild.

"Have a look for them, boys, while I keep this half-breed busy," the alpha coyote huffed. But he had underestimated the mule's resolve. With a bray that echoed off the mountain walls, he rushed at the coyote.

The next few seconds were a blur of teeth and fur and the rage of stomping feet. Max dropped to the ground, hoping to avoid a random kick to the head from the mule's hooves. As quickly as it had started, the battle was over. The coyotes ran for the trees, yipping all the way, with the mule braying after them at the top of his lungs.

"And stay out of my valley, if you know what's good for you!"

Nostrils flaring wildly, the mule turned his angry eyes toward Max.

"Do you need some help moving along, mutt?" the

mule asked the cowering dog.

"Um, I'm not with them," Max said, belly to the ground. "I live up at the top of the mountain with some humans."

"Coyote assassin or bored house dog, makes no difference to me. Get out of my valley!" the mule bellowed and ran at Max with those giant teeth chomping at the air.

Out of options, Max ran in the same direction as the coyotes, with the mule close behind making sure he didn't stop. The dog quickly outran the enraged mule and flopped down in the grass to catch his breath.

Running for his life was a new experience, but his heart thumping in his chest and his blood flowing at high speed reminded him that he was not so far removed from his shaggy canine cousins.

He heard snickering from the edge of the forest. Lifting his head, Max noticed that the trio of coyotes was watching him.

"So, are you coming?" the alpha asked him. "Dinner isn't going to just walk up and smack you in the face."

Max had never needed to hunt for his food.

Breakfast and dinner were always served in a big metal dish. He loved to play at hunting and was an expert at killing stuffed toys. He could carry them gently in his mouth like his Labrador instincts told him to, but he could also chew a tiny hole in the fur and gut out all the stuffing like an expert.

The foster lady who raised him was not impressed by this talent and warned the Mama-lady before she took him home. She rarely gave him a chance to show off his skills. But one day Max had accidently gotten left out on a chilly, rainy day, and Mama had given him a toy to rip up, as an apology. That was an excellent day.

He wasn't really hungry right that minute. Dinner had been served in his big metal dish in a timely manner. But the chance to run wild with the coyotes on a moonlit spring night was too exciting to pass up. He was sure he could be an excellent hunter if he had the chance. And who knows what coyotes will get into in the forest at night?

"Yes. Definitely, yes," Max said, still catching his breath. "I'm right behind you."

ON THE TRAIL

Max took great pride in his nose. Every morning he scoured his mountaintop and took stock of every creature, great and small, that had visited during the night. Deer, rabbit, skunk, armadillo, raccoon, snake, squirrel, possum, lizard, roadrunner—nothing escaped his notice. He was sure that he was the most excellent sniffer in the Ozarks. That is, until he tried to keep up with the coyotes.

Their lives depended on their noses. It was no contest.

"Rabbit," the alpha coyote snorted, sniffing at the air moments after Max joined them, and the four of them were off.

Max followed along through the tall trees, trying to look busy and on-the-scent, but he couldn't even find the trail. Dead leaves crunched under their trotting paws. Unseen creatures scuttled away in the darkness, but the coyotes didn't break their concentration. The lead dog was confident with their path, so Max just followed the white-and-brown swish of tail ahead of him in the moonlight.

With a yip, the lead coyote took off. He was out of sight in the trees in a flash, but his partners kept moving forward at a gentle trot. In a moment, the leader returned, but there was no rabbit in his jaws.

"Got away," he mumbled. The other two snorted their understanding and began sniffing the air again.

"Smell anything?" the leader asked Max, his eyes narrowing. He wouldn't normally allow a dog to join them on their nightly hunt, but they could use all the help they could get on the mountain these days. Scoring a calf hadn't worked out. *Stupid mule. Maybe this lazy house dog can be of some use,* he thought.

Max tried to concentrate and find a good trail, but, frankly, all he smelled was the dank odor of the coyotes. He couldn't think of a polite way to admit that, so he just lowered his head and snuffled around in the leaves. Telling these wild dogs that their odor was stronger than anything around didn't seem like a wise move. If they were to turn on him, it would also not even be a contest. Staying alive and in one piece was a better plan. Max could uncover other odors deep in the leaves, but none were fresh enough to start a hunt.

The woods were silent, except for the occasional hoot of an owl and the snuffling sounds from the four hunters. Breaking the silence, an ambulance or police siren wailed from the highway that wound through the mountains. The piercing sound echoed through the valley and the trees. The coyotes locked eyes, and the leader chortled in delight. Then the three of them lifted their snouts to the sky and let loose howls that made Max's skin tingle from the tips of his ears to the tip of his tail.

The noise surged through every wild fiber of his being, but he didn't dare join in. Like the abilities of his nose, Max was pretty sure his howl would fall short of the unearthly sounds coming from his wild cousins. Their howls were high pitched and loud and rang through the valley—sounding almost exactly like the siren wail.

When they finally lowered their heads, the coyotes smiled at each other, and one of the smaller ones hopped around in the leaves in pure delight. The alpha raised his head once more and threw out a howl even louder and more blood-curdling. From far away in another valley, the howls and yips of other coyotes floated back to them. The alpha gave a satisfied snort.

"I wonder how Cheyenne has fared in the hunt tonight?" he said.

The four of them listened as the faraway group of coyotes howled and yipped along with the ambulance siren.

"Cheyenne is my mate," the leader said, focusing his intent brown eyes on Max. "Do you have a mate?"

"No," Max admitted. "I just have lots of cats."

The coyotes exchanged looks that Max thought were more confused than approving.

"I am Winema. Leader," the alpha coyote said. "This is Kaliska and Yutu. My mate and our pack hunt separately from us tonight because the moon is full and we might catch a deer with the extra light to guide us. Then we can gather and share. Have you ever hunted a deer, Dog?"

"No, but I have followed their trail into the woods before from my mountain." He was proud that at least he had some experience to offer. "My owner never lets me get far enough away to really trail them far."

"Maybe you should rejoin your human," Winema said. "Are you lost, Dog?"

Max smelled the air and looked at the woods around him. There was no sign of home or any landmarks he recognized.

"I suppose I am lost," he admitted, "but I'm not really interested in going back. I ran off on purpose. And it's Max. The humans call me Max."

"Very well, Max. But we don't go near humans. We might grab a calf or a sheep or two when the hunting is scarce or maybe when the moon is bright and we are in the mood, like tonight in that mule's territory."

Winema snorted with annoyance, and the other two snorted back at him. "But humans are to be avoided at all costs."

"Dogs are to be avoided too," Yutu huffed under his breath.

The three coyotes locked eyes, and Max felt that wild tension emanate from them again. He suddenly wondered if it had been a bad decision to follow these untamed creatures so far away into the woods. If they were to turn on him, he might make a nice dinner too. He was certainly no match for three trained hunters. He struggled to keep his hackles down as fear raced along his spine. Being submissive was the only way to survive in a house full of cats and humans, but in that moonlit moment, instinct told him that any sign of weakness was very, very dangerous.

"Dogs normally mean humans are not far off. Or wild dogs may want to compete for food. Do you want to take our dinner away, Max the Dog?"

"That seems like a very dumb thing to try to do," Max said.

The three coyotes looked content with that answer.

"And will you share your kill with the pack?" Winema asked. Max couldn't imagine that he would kill something before one of the coyotes, but he nodded agreement. "Individuals in the pack are welcome to snap up little animals for their own meals, but if we find a deer tonight, everyone must share. And Cheyenne and I eat first," Winema said firmly.

The other two coyotes lowered their heads, so Max did the same as well. Winema flicked his tall ears in satisfaction, but then he turned his head toward more yips and howls from the other valley.

"Cheyenne has found a trail," Yutu said, eyes sparkling.

"Sounds like an injured deer," Kaliska said, panting in excitement.

"Come," Winema yipped, and the coyotes took off at a brisk trot to join the pack.

Max tried his best to keep up. The moon couldn't brighten up the forest where the trees grew close together. Locking in on the scent of Winema, Max swerved and dodged to avoid evergreen and thick maple trunks. His foot caught on an exposed root, but he leapt up quickly and rejoined the group. Branches flapped back and slapped him in the face. Try as he may, Max couldn't stay with them. It seemed like they were going mostly uphill. Cheyenne and the others of their pack were in another valley, so up and over was the shortest route.

As the trees thinned near the top of the mountain, Max caught the distinctive odor of the highway. Concrete and gasoline mixed with metallic and human odors. As the group moved out of hiding in the trees, the coyotes broke into a flat out run—right across the highway.

Max expected to follow them. He really did. But as he raced close to the edge of the road the training in his head could not be outrun. The Daddy-man's warnings echoed in his mind louder than the coyote's ambulance howl.

No, Max!

Highways are bad. Stay!

Never, never go into the road!

Bad Dog, Max!!

Max skidded to a stop in the gravel, his strong back

feet spraying rocks out all around him, and sat down at the side of the road. The coyotes had already vanished into the trees on the other side.

Max couldn't hear any cars, but lessons that had been drilled into him made his legs freeze. When the Daddy-man made the long walk down the driveway to get the mail from the metal box right next to the road, he made Max sit and wait farther up the driveway.

Stay.

He didn't use that word often, but he meant it when he did. The dog had seen the cars and massive trucks speed by and had never questioned the order to wait. Highways were dangerous.

This two-lane road was nothing compared to the giant highways that Max remembered from when they lived in the big city in Texas, but it still had its share of fast-moving traffic. *Zoom.* Max had watched them race past and been glad he was far away. Some of the big trucks made horrible, metal-grinding noises as they reached the top of his mountain and prepared for the steep, winding descent back down the other side.

A silly dog named Dusty that lived on the other side of the highway liked to dart across to come visit Max sometimes, but the Daddy-man always watched carefully to be sure that Max never returned the favor. And he led Dusty carefully back across the road to make sure he was safe from cars.

Standing by the roadside in the moonlight alone, Max didn't have a human to guide him, but he knew what the Daddy-man would say.

Stay. Good Dog.

He didn't have to follow the human rules now. Wasn't he free and wild with the whole world ahead of him? Wild and tame instincts wrestled through him. If he was just careful and listened for cars, he could certainly make it across the road. There was no Daddy-man watching now. Max the Dog was free!

He sniffed the air, wondering if he could find a trail for the coyote pack. Maybe they had stopped on the other side of the road, just hidden in the trees, to wait for him. He couldn't find a whiff of them.

Max heard yipping noises echo up to him at the top of the mountain, but it was hard to distinguish if they were from Winema and his buddies or Cheyenne and her group in the valley. Sounds do funny things in the Ozark Mountains.

As he contemplated risking his life and dashing across to try to find them, headlights shone on Max's black fur. He caught the rancid smell of fuel and metal and heard the grinding of gears that the huge semis make as they try to crest the mountain.

Vrrrooommm. Kkerrrkkk. Vrrrooomm. Kkerrrkkk.

The sharp metallic noises pained his sensitive ears.

Max backed into the trees to hide so the driver wouldn't see him. The huge truck blasted past in a billow of gagging smoke and the acrid smell of a dozen tires pulling at the road. Max snorted twice to clear his poor nose. *Snerk. Snerk!*

Yes, highways were dangerous, and smelly, but he also realized that unless the coyotes turned back to find him, he would never catch up. Those hunters were on a trail. They weren't coming back. He was all alone again. Max sat down in the grass and dead leaves at the edge of the woods and wondered what in the world he was going to do next.

The coyotes locked eyes, and the leader chortled in delight. Then the three of them lifted their snouts to the sky and let loose howls that made Max's skin tingle from the tips of his ears to the tip of his tail.

5

HOUSE IN THE WOODS

Max had never had so many options open to him before. Most of his daily decisions were no more complicated than which human to follow, whether that unfamiliar sound outside required him to bark and alert the household, or where to take a nap. Being wild and free required a lot of thought.

Should he make a mad dash across the highway like the coyotes and try to find them? He was sure he could pick up their trail, but they moved so much faster than he could in the dark woods. Chasing a deer with his new wild friends sounded exciting, but when he thought about what would happen when they caught it, he felt a lump in his throat. Following a trail was instinctive. Herding and chasing and retrieving was vital based on lessons deeply imprinted in his DNA. Actually killing things was not. Killing an animal was a major *Bad Dog* for any Border Collie. Max knew he could never do it.

Another option, going back into the forest, was only a little bit more appealing than hunting deer. All alone, he noticed creaky noises that he hadn't before. The moon lit things up nicely out in the open, but in the trees his nose was his only guide. And his nose told him there were lots of other creatures moving around in there. Back into the woods didn't sound like such a great idea until the sun came out.

Well then, should he follow the road uphill and see where it led? When he went for walks with the Daddy-man, up was always the way back home. Max had no interest in going back home. Home wasn't interesting at all. That left only one option: downhill along the road. Attempting a snort like his departed coyote friends, Max began to work his way down the mountain.

There wasn't much of a shoulder on the road along the steep mountain passes, so Max walked along slowly. He picked his way around sharp rocks and roadside bushes, being sure to stay clear of the concrete of the road. He was pretty sure he would hear any machines before they got to him, but he had never tried that theory and didn't feel like testing it too much that night.

After he had walked what felt like about halfway down the mountain, Max noticed one of those metal mailboxes that humans got so excited about and a gravel driveway like his own, leading off the highway. Exploring the area, Max could distinguish the smells of more than one dog—two or three maybe—and two humans. The trails were faint, but they clearly led up the driveway and into the darkness.

Should he stop and explore? The humans were sure to be asleep. Certainly not outside. And Max's tummy was beginning to grumble a bit. He didn't normally do this much climbing and running and chasing after dinner. Maybe he could find something to munch on. If he wasn't going to kill things for food, Max realized he was going to have to get creative about where his next meals would come from. That was the first hitch in his plans for freedom. Free and wild meant that no one handed you breakfast and dinner in a big metal bowl. His tummy rumbled again. Up the driveway he went, in search of a snack.

Trotting in the grass alongside the gravel driveway was easier on the paws, and Max picked up the scent of one dog who must have done the exact same thing. It led him along a winding path, much longer than his own driveway back home, and into the heavy trees of the forest. Just when he began to wonder if it was actually a road to nowhere, he trotted into a large clearing with a small, white house in the middle of it.

The roof of the house glimmered and shone in the bright moonlight. That seemed odd, but Max soon recognized blocks of glass-like material all over the roof. Solar panels, like his house had, but many, many more of them. The Daddy-man was very proud of the few solar panels his house had as a back-up in case the power went out. What would he think of this place in the woods? The whole roof was one giant solar energy capturing machine!

The Daddy-man would be impressed by this, for sure, Max thought. Then his heart felt unexpectedly heavy. He shook his head with a snort. Missing humans was no way for a wild and free dog to behave.

The windows in the house were dark. Everyone was asleep, like he had expected, but he could smell faint odors of food lingering in the air. Maybe there was still some leftover dinner somewhere. Max trotted around the front yard but found nothing, so he headed toward the back of the house.

Walking boldly around the corner, Max suddenly found himself confronted by an enormous black dog. He stood nearly a head taller than Max, and his broad chest looked like it could withstand a wrecking ball.

At the same time, they both jumped and planted their feet wide on the ground in a defensive position. Locking eyes, Max couldn't decide if this strange dog was angry or just as surprised as he was. Who knew some dogs slept outside at night?

Now in a standoff, Max wondered if coming up this driveway had been an even worse idea than following the coyotes. A dog protecting his yard at night was a force to be reckoned with. He felt his hackles rise as fear spread down his back.

6

ODIN AND THOR

Instinct told Max not to break eye contact. Looking away could signal a weakness and make the enormous black dog attack. Sniffing at the air, he could also smell another dog nearby. Running might be an option. He sure couldn't take on this big dog, much less any others who might join the fight. The solar panel house dog was not snarling or threatening, just staring, so Max tried to talk his way out of it.

"Hey," he said casually.

"Hey, yourself," the black dog answered.

No snarl. No growl. Be cool. Be cool.

"Didn't mean to surprise you," Max said as calmly as he could manage, his nose still madly attempting to determine if anyone might be coming up behind him.

Staring the black dog in the face, he noticed that his muzzle and jowls were turning grey. Enormous, *old* black dog, he corrected his first impression, but that didn't make the guard dog any less dangerous. An angry dog defending his yard was still an angry dog defending his yard. Teeth were still teeth.

"We get lots of visitors, but never in the middle of the night," the black dog said. "Where's your human?"

"What makes you think I have a human? I'm all alone."

The black dog broke eye contact and looked Max up and down.

"You clearly have a human. Your fur is clean. Your toe nails are trimmed. You are well fed. Definitely a human in the mix."

"Definitely," a sharp voice said from the darkness. "He has pet written all over him, Odin."

Max lifted his ears. That must be the other dog.

Max couldn't see him, but he was grateful to know that he wasn't sneaking up from behind somewhere.

"Okay, so I did have a human," Max admitted. "I ran away tonight."

"Ran away?" Odin said, breaking his defensive stance and sitting down hard. "Why in the world would you run away? Was your human cruel?"

"No, no," Max said quickly.

"Did he forget to feed you?"

"No, no, nothing like that," Max insisted.

"He's an ungrateful pet," the other dog growled from the darkness. "Bite him, Odin. Bite him now. Drive him away."

Odin considered Max, but didn't move. Suspicion was creeping in. Max could sense Odin's growing concern and fear over a dog who doesn't appreciate his humans.

"Kill him," the voice from the darkness barked wildly. "Kill him now."

Max jumped back to a defensive position, his hackles at full attention at threats like that, but Odin didn't move.

"Calm down, Thor," he said. "We haven't heard the whole story. Maybe this former pet would like to explain himself."

Being free and wild was a threat to these dogs. Max could feel it. Odin was impressive in size, even if he was old, and Thor was apparently lurking in the shadows. *Thor?* Max had watched those movies with the family.

If a dog like Thor wants me dead, what chance do I have here alone in the woods at night? Max wondered. Quick thinking and some side stepping were necessary.

"I got lost," Max said, trying to sound sad and sheepish. Being lost should earn him some pity, but Odin did not seem impressed.

"I thought you said you ran away."

"Kill him," the unseen Thor snarled.

"I took off after the trail of a strange animal so I could find out what it looked like," he said, "but then I realized I had gotten far away from my house." He left out the part about the Daddy-man calling for him and running away instead of being obedient. Odin seemed to know there was more to the story. He stared at Max, still unmoving as stone.

"Oh, what are you waiting for, Odin?" Thor barked from the shadows. "Kill him! Kill him! KILL HIM!"

In his excitement over Max's imminent death, Thor bounced into the moonlight and stood next to Odin. At the sight of him, Max was too astounded to run or growl or say anything at all.

KILLER DOG

From what Max had witnessed on TV, Thor was a god from another planet who had a magical hammer that could smash up anything and everything without a second thought. Thor was a mighty warrior. Thor was nearly invincible.

However, the Thor that wanted him dead on this full-moon night in the middle of the Ozark woods was not like that. This Thor looked more like a messy cat than a dog. He barely came up to Odin's knees, and his white spiky hair stuck out at odd angles all over his very tiny, very skinny body.

Talk about all bark and no bite, Max thought.

"If you're not gonna kill him, then I'll handle it," Thor growled. "Ungrateful curs that run away from perfectly good humans must die! Death to all trespassers! Kill! Kill! Kill!" he yipped.

"Calm down," Odin said without even looking at his partner. "Master will not be happy if you wake him up over a lost dog." He examined Max from head to toe again. "Besides, death seems like a pretty stiff penalty for a pet who is simply separated from home."

"Killlll..." Thor grumbled in his chest.

Max didn't want to laugh in the little dog's face, but death threats from whatever kind of miniature, mangy-type dog this was in front of him were hard to take seriously. Then he remembered some tangles he had gotten into with the cats at home.

The spotted one, the little monster that the Mama-lady called her tiny cheetah, had attached her whole body to Max's face once when he tried to break up a feline disagreement. Tiny could still mean vicious. Mini-Thor didn't have claws like a cat, but he did still have some nasty little sharp teeth in his mouth.

Ticking him off further was probably not a good idea.

"What is your given name?" Odin asked him with a tilt of his head.

"Max. The humans called me Max when I was born, before I was left at the shelter with my brothers and sisters. Then the Mama-lady came and took me home with her a year later. She calls me Max too."

"You must be very grateful to this human for giving you a safe, warm home to call your own."

"Yes, Sir." Max found himself swallowing the lump in his throat. He should be grateful. He knew he should. But there were so many rules and so much fuss and bother and worry and responsibility.

"So, do you need help finding your home again, Max?" Odin asked calmly—but with a stern tinge that made Max pretty sure that he'd better answer *Yes*.

"It is at the top of one of these mountains. That's all I know."

"Maybe you should stay here for the night and our master can help you find your way home in the morning. I see you have perfectly good tags hanging from your collar. Many dogs get lost in these woods.

We always help them find their way home."

"No. Kill him," Thor whispered, his eyes bright and shining in the moonlight.

"Now, Thor, that would not be showing much compassion or Southern hospitality, would it? What would the master say?"

"Kill him."

"No, he most certainly would not," Odin sighed. "You will have to forgive my friend here. He may be small of stature, but he is mighty of heart."

Thor glared at Max, his lips curling and uncurling in a threatening snarl. Max thought back on a hot summer day when he and the Daddy-man were walking around a lake back at their Texas home. A long, tiny Dachshund had run up to them and barked all kinds of threats like a crazy creature, for no good reason whatsoever. One *whooff* from Max was all it had taken to send that little dog yipeing and running for home. What was it about tiny dogs that made them so aggressive?

He could probably do that to Thor now. One. Big. *Whooff.* It would have felt wonderfully satisfying, but

49

Odin didn't look like he would be amused.

"I understand," was all Max said, but he *whooffed* at the little dog in his mind.

"You must be exhausted," Odin said. "You can rest here safely with us for the night. We stand guard for our master. The little ones need protecting from coyotes and foxes and such."

"Kill them all," Thor muttered, as he spun in a circle three times and plopped down on the ground. He seemed resigned to the fact that Max would be allowed to see the sunrise. Any other creature who ventured onto this property should still beware.

Max had been so focused on the two dogs that he had not noticed the cages behind them in the dark. Focusing his nose in that direction, he was overwhelmed with unfamiliar smells. A large red feather blew toward him and landed at his feet.

"What's back there?" Max asked.

"Haven't you ever seen a chicken coop?" Odin wondered.

He stepped aside so Max had a clearer view of the cages. The birds inside looked like short-legged, fat roadrunners. No, more like smaller versions of the turkeys that fed on the acorns in the yard in the fall. The Daddy-man got very upset when Max chased those stupid turkeys, but boy did they look silly when they tried to outrun him. *Bad Dog, Max.* He wondered what those chickens would look like running for their lives. Not sure what Max was thinking, Odin cleared his throat.

"Thor and I will do everything in our power to protect these little ones. It is our responsibility. It is the command of our master. Do you understand?" He looked Max dead in the eyes.

Yes, Max understood. Thor's chant of *kill, kill* would be carried out by Odin if Max made a move on the chickens. Very Bad Dog. He understood, but he could still imagine it.

"You can sleep here, and our master will get you home when the sun rises," Odin said. Then he returned to a favorite hollowed-out spot on the ground next to the chicken coop. That must have been where he was waiting when Max first rounded the corner. He swallowed hard. It was a good thing Odin didn't just attack first and ask questions later. A chicken would make a very good meal for a hungry, lost dog. His stomach growled again. Odin noticed.

"Sorry," Max said. "Dinner is usually enough, but this has been a busy night."

"I'm sorry too," Odin said, "because we have nothing to offer. Leaving food out at night only attracts undesirable creatures." He didn't add, *like you*, but Max was pretty sure he thought it.

Odin and Thor settled into their guarding positions, but Max wasn't sure what to do next. He was confident that the two dogs were not sleeping. They were on duty, even if their eyes were closed. If he stayed, their master would read his tags and take him back home in the morning.

Did he want to go back home? There was easy food at home. That was true. But nothing else had changed, and Max had not done much exploring and living at all. Wild and free still won out in his heart. But how was he going to slip away from them now?

Before he could figure that part out, Odin's eyes snapped open and a low growl rumbled through his body. Thor leapt to his tiny feet, every hair on full alert. Max thought they sensed that he was going to run and were angry, but neither dog was looking at him. Following Odin's gaze into the darkness, Max saw two yellow, glowing eyes.

They were not alone.

8

SKUNKZILLA

Max tested the air, but he couldn't smell anything new. The eyes blinked and winked in the darkness. They were coming closer. Max felt his hackles rise all the way up the back of his neck. Could it be Winema the coyote and his mate? Had they followed him here? No, the eyes were too low to the ground to be a coyote or a dog. Maybe a fox? Max had never met a fox. Whatever it was, the anger and aggressive energy flowing off Odin and Thor was enough to make him put up his guard as well.

"What is it?" he whispered to Odin. "I can't smell anything at all."

"Danger," Odin snarled.

"How can you tell if you don't know what it is?"

"That's my job. It is my supreme duty in this world. Protect the helpless little ones. Obey the master. Whatever that is, it is coming toward the little ones in the dark. That is never good."

Odin snarled again, a bit louder this time. The eyes stopped moving and blinked on and off a few times.

"Killlll…" Thor growled.

Rising from the ground, Odin planted his feet in a wide, defensive stance, lowered his head, and bared his teeth in warning.

"Who's out there?" he growled.

"It's just little old me," a grumbly voice answered. "Nothing for you to worry about."

"That's for me to decide," Odin said. "Show yourself."

The bright eyes blinked a few more times, then came closer. All three dogs were now at full attention. Just because the creature said it wasn't dangerous didn't mean it wasn't. Wild instinct told them all to be ready. Soon the animal waddled out into the moonlight and a waft of its scent hit Max. He had never seen or smelled anything like it.

At first, he was ready to run. It looked like a skunk. It had the same black body and face with white-and-black stripes of fur, but it was three times the size of most skunks he had ever seen. *A really huge skunk?* There was no way he was going to tangle with a skunk again. But it didn't smell like a skunk. Confused, Max looked to Odin, but he had not changed his posture at all. Maybe he was crazy-obedient enough to take on Skunkzilla to protect those chickens.

"What business do you have here?" Odin demanded of the giant skunk creature.

"Well," the creature mumbled, "I'm just exploring and looking for some dinner."

This made Odin curl his lips back further and sent Thor into a rage.

"Kill! Kill! Kill! Kill!"

"Now, now," the creature said, "that can hardly be necessary. I'm just a humble little badger. I'm not any trouble to you big, strong dogs. You stay where you are, and I'll just amble on along over here. I already see what I was looking for."

"And what's that, Badger?" Odin said, not relaxing a muscle.

"Well, dinner, of course. And it's exactly where my friend Winema the wise and wily and wonderful coyote said it would be. Here chicky, chicky, chicky. Ohhh, yummy, yummy, yummy little chicky, chicky, chicky."

The badger started to waddle his way closer to the far end of the chicken coop. That was the last straw for Odin. With Thor dancing and snapping at his side, the old black dog ran at the badger, teeth snapping. Startled, the badger stumbled back and bared his own teeth as well, hissing.

"No one touches the chickens," Odin growled. "Not you, and not that mangy old coyote."

"Now, now, now," the badger grumbled, trying to stand his ground, "there's no need for name calling. Winema was just trying to help me out. Dinner has been so scarce lately. Maybe I could just have a couple of eggs? One or two?"

The badger took another step toward the coop, but this time Odin let loose the full horror of his barking arsenal. Foam leapt from his snapping jaws, and the badger staggered backward again, teeth bared. Max wasn't sure if he should join in or run away. That badger with his sharp teeth and claws looked dangerous enough if it came down to outright combat.

A light switched on in the house, and it caught the immediate attention of both Max and the badger. A human, the master, had heard the commotion. Odin had done his job well. Thor had probably helped a bit too. The back door to the house swung open, and a gray-haired man in baggy pajamas stumbled out into the night.

Max ran for the shadows closer to the house, but the badger stayed frozen in place. Odin and Thor continued their tirade, even louder now that they had backup. A loud metallic clunk came from the direction of the master, and Max realized that he had a gun. A big shotgun. The badger saw it too. That was the end of the conversation. The badger scuttled off into the darkness without looking back.

"What's out there, Odin?" the man hollered over the barking.

Odin calmed himself to a low growl and yelled to the retreating badger, "And don't bother coming back!"

"Kill, Kill, Kiiilllll!"

With the badger now gone, Odin relaxed and sat down. All his old dog energy was spent. The master walked over to him and patted him gently on the head.

"Good dog. Good dog," he mumbled sleepily. Thor hopped around his feet for acknowledgement as well. "Yes, you too, Thor. Good dogs."

Watching the master praise Odin made Max's heart ache a bit. The Daddy-man never praised him for barking at animals in the yard. He just got annoyed. "Leave it, Max," was the most he would say. Didn't he know that Max was only trying to protect the family like Odin was protecting the chickens?

Now that all was calm, Odin looked around the yard until he found Max hiding in the shadows. He ambled over to him and sat down.

"What ya got there, Odin?" the man asked, following him.

Max contemplated running, but he was scared the man would shoot if he thought he was another badger or a coyote. Being found seemed safer.

"Well, what have we here?" the master said. "You lost, boy?"

The man reached out his hand for Max to sniff, which he did like a Good Dog should. Then he allowed the man to pat his head and look at the tags on his collar. He couldn't quite read them in the dark, so he pulled a little flashlight out of his pocket.

"You didn't get too far," the man said. "The address sounds like it's just back up the road a few miles. Hang out here for the night. We'll get ya back home in the morning, just like we always do. We always get 'em home again, don't we, Odin?"

The old dog snorted and leaned against the man. He patted his head again.

"Good Boy, Odin."

Then the man shone the flashlight around the yard, checking for other intruders, as he wandered toward the house and back to bed. Odin watched his master go, his barrel of a chest swelling with pride. Then he headed back over to his favorite, worn-out dirt spot and curled back up to rest.

"That's a good night's work," he said.

"Should have killed it," Thor grumbled, moving back into his spot as well. "Should have killed you," he said to Max.

"Simmer down, you monster," Odin teased. "Our job isn't to kill. It's to protect and warn the master of real danger to the little ones and our home."

Thor mumbled something Max couldn't quite hear, but it made Odin chuckle. It was probably about killing something. Max felt a huge yawn struggling to get out. *Awwrrwwwwnn.* It broke free and made Thor grumble at him again.

"You can find a spot to relax if you want," Odin said, "but we don't really sleep much until morning. Most dangers come in the dark around here."

"Sorry, I usually spend all night in the house in my crate sound asleep."

Odin and Thor exchanged glances.

"Good thing you escaped from that torture and misery," Thor said. Max was pretty sure that he didn't mean it.

"Living with the humans and protecting them and all that is a part of your domain is a solemn duty. It must never be forsaken or taken lightly," Odin said.

"The Daddy-man, my master, doesn't like me to bark at animals. Or the mailman. Or the delivery men. I guess he doesn't appreciate barking much," Max admitted.

"Well, that is a sad state of things," Odin agreed.

"Still, I should probably head back that way. He must be worried by now. Your master said my house is back up the road, so if I just follow the highway up the mountain I should end up home again soon."

Max had no intention of going back, but it was an easy solution for how to get away from serious old Odin and homicidal miniature Thor. Once he hit the end of the driveway, the dogs would have no idea where he went from there.

"You could just cut through the forest," Thor suggested with a snarl. "Nothing dangerous out there at all. Nothing that could KILL you." The little dog chuckled deep in his throat, but it got caught and came out more like a snergly cough.

"Whatever you do, don't head into the woods that way," Odin said, looking toward the west. "When master and I were walking that way a few weeks ago, I could smell cats. Lots of cats. Cats that didn't smell like they answer to humans."

"Wild cats, like cougars or bobcats?" Max asked. Wild cats were dangerous and to be avoided at all costs. He was grateful to never even have smelled one.

"No. Worse."

"Worse than a cougar?" Max shuddered.

"A cougar will kill ya quick," Thor muttered.

"Give it a rest, Thor," Odin said. "And, yes. Worse than a cougar. Feral cats. Cats that should be housecats but refuse to be. They are more dangerous than any cougar or bobcat because they don't follow the rules. They are reckless and usually a bit crazy. This group smelled odd. I've never smelled anything like it. Don't go that way."

"Understood," Max said with a quick nod of his

head. Tame cats were enough to make any dog crazy. Unruly wild cats were best avoided in a big wide arch. "I think I'll just stick to the highway. Then I won't risk getting lost again."

Odin considered this plan and seemed to find it acceptable to his idea of how the dog and human world should work. Yes, Max should get back home as soon as possible. It was only logical.

"Good luck, then," he said. "And stay out of the road, whatever you do."

"Absolutely," Max agreed. "Try to get some sleep."

"Not until morning," Odin said, resting his head on his front paws.

"Goodbye, Thor," Max said, to be polite.

The little dog grumbled and curled up into an even tinier ball. He would probably dream of killing Max.

Before Odin could change his mind, Max trotted back around the house and down the driveway.

Good Dog, Odin thought as Max headed out.

But he was wrong. When Max hit the end of the driveway and was back at the highway again, he didn't hesitate. He headed down the mountain, away from home, instead of up.

It had the same black body and face with white-and-black stripes of fur, but it was three times the size of most skunks he had ever seen.

9

ESCAPING THE COLLAR

Max was shocked to discover that he hadn't really traveled that far in the last few hours. Chasing the coyotes through the woods had made it feel like he was far, far away from all of those rules and responsibilities, but they were still right up the road. If he had stayed at the solar panel house, the master would have just taken him back home in the morning.

It was his collar. That collar branded him a pet with a home, instead of a wild and free dog with no humans to answer to. He had only been without a collar a few times in his life. When he was just a newborn puppy, of course.

Once, when the Mama-lady was walking him, right after she had brought him home from the shelter, Max had slipped out of his collar and left her holding the leash and calling for him helplessly. Max stopped walking down the mountain and closed his eyes.

That had been an amazing few minutes. He had flat out run down the sidewalks and all around the neighborhood, not worrying about streets or corners or heeling or any other leash rules. He had raced past some men who were working with leaf blowers and lawn edgers. They looked back at the Mama-lady chasing him and laughed.

"El hombre," one of them muttered with pride.

Max wasn't sure what it meant, but he was pretty sure they were impressed with his speed and agility. Nothing could stop him! It was the most wild and wonderful feeling of his entire life.

Then he had smelled it: the bacon-flavored treats that the Mama-lady kept in her pockets. She was calling to him from across the street. What could it hurt to just take one little, amazing, delicious treat?

That was the day that Max learned that a treat was also a trap. *Snip snap* and the Mama-lady had him back on a leash. Captivity again. The Mama-lady had sighed and sat down on a nearby bench to catch her breath. The lawn guys shook their heads sadly.

"Pobre muchacho."

Poor guy.

Those men had understood. A dog needs to run free.

Now he was as free as he had been that day, running wild in his Texas neighborhood, but the collar and tags dangling around his neck were a one-way ticket back to the house. There had to be some way to get it off. Max looked around, but there was nothing but the highway on one side and the forest on the other. His collar wasn't on very tight these days because they didn't need a leash to go walking on their property. Maybe he could just rub it off.

Max leaned on a nearby tree and rubbed the side of his neck along the bark. *Gack*. He nearly choked. Wrong way. That was just jamming it on further.

Leaning against the tree again, he stepped backwards. The collar caught on the bark and began to slip up, up over his head. That was very exciting until he realized that it wasn't moving any farther. It was stuck part way. Now, instead of being around his neck, the collar was under his chin and over one ear.

Panic set in. What if he was trapped like that forever now? Dropping to the rocky ground, Max rolled and pawed and slid his way along. At one point he ended up with the collar still stuck over his head, but his front paw was wedged in there as well. Now he couldn't walk! Wrestle and struggle and rub on the ground as he might, he was still trapped in the collar.

Regretting even starting this great escape attempt, Max would have even been happy just to get the collar back around his neck. It was all becoming hopeless, and a car or truck might come along at any minute and spot him. Even at night, the highway was never quiet for long. Rolling onto his back, Max gave one more mighty heave, and *snap*, the clasp of the collar came loose, and he was free.

Max lay there for a minute, gasping for air. That had been way more intense than he had expected, but it was done. Now there was no link to his home up the mountain. No one would ever know to take him back there. He rolled onto his side, not feeling nearly as satisfied as he thought he would be.

There was nothing to link him to his home. It was permanent. If a human caught him, he would just be another stray dog loose in the mountains. The reality of that left a hollow feeling in the pit of his stomach. His very empty stomach. It growled to remind him that no one was going to plop a meal into a metal bowl for him this time.

Now that he was free of the collar, for better or for worse, he was going to have to come up with something to eat. Those chickens were starting to sound mighty tasty right about now. Drool pooled up in his mouth, remembering the badger's *chicky, chicky, chicky, yummy, yummy, yummy.* He was pretty sure he wasn't capable of killing a chicken though. Not yet, at least. His tummy grumbled again. No. Not just yet. But maybe not too long from now.

What will I be willing to do if I don't find a meal soon? he thought.

NEW FRIENDS

At the bottom of the mountain where the ground leveled off, the highway continued on into the darkness. Max had been in a car past this point. The groomer that shaved off his fur in the summer, gave him baths, trimmed his toenails, cleaned his ears, and did other unmentionable things to him was farther down that road. Max shuddered at the thought. As a wild and free dog, he would never have to go to the groomer again. His coat would be long and shaggy, like the Mama-lady let it grow in the winter. *Winter?* Max shook his head. Winter was something to worry about later. Right now, he had places to explore.

Not too far down the road, he spotted an old building that looked abandoned. Checking the area for scents, Max thought he smelled dogs. Very aromatic dogs. Dogs could mean humans, and he was beginning to understand the coyotes' reasons for avoiding strange humans. They might try to trap you or worse if they thought you were messing with their stuff. Max approached carefully, checking with his nose every few minutes as the dog smells got closer.

"Go!" a hidden dog barked.

Max jumped in alarm, but the order had nothing to do with him. A scruffy brown dog raced past him and across the highway. He stopped on the other side and barked wildly.

"Did it! See! I'm no chicken!"

From out of the building, two other dogs laughed and stepped into the moonlight. Max was pretty sure they hadn't seen him yet, so he froze in place.

"You idiot!" a filthy yellow dog said. "You didn't even check for cars first."

"Naw," the daredevil brown dog said. "Ya just gotta move fast. They can't hit ya if you're moving fast."

"That is the stupidest thing I ever heard you say," the yellow dog said, sitting down by the road. "And you say a lot of stupid things." The other dog laughed in agreement, shaking his matted red fur.

"If you're paying attention," the red dog said, "ya don't even have to move fast."

He sauntered out into the road, meandering around instead of crossing over. He sat down right on the yellow middle line and scratched his ear.

"I tell ya, it's all about paying attention."

At that moment, Max noticed headlights coming up the mountain road. They were coming straight for the crazy red dog, but he was looking at his buddies and definitely not paying attention.

"Look out!" Max barked. "CAR!"

He ran toward the group on the roadside, but the red dog was frozen in the middle of the road, now staring at the approaching headlights.

"Carl! Get out of there!" the yellow dog barked, but Carl didn't move.

The other dogs began barking wildly, but none of it affected Carl. Max couldn't stand it. His Border Collie instinct flew into high gear. An animal was in trouble. An animal needed direction and saving. Without thinking it through any further, Max rushed out into the road and grabbed Carl by the scruff of the neck. Using every ounce of his strength, Max dragged the now limp dog out of the road and back toward his friends.

Whoosh, the car raced by. Their fur blasted flat against their bodies as the wind from the car hit them.

Hooonnnk! The driver blared his horn, realizing he just missed running them both over. Max hadn't gotten Carl totally out of the road, but he was clear of oncoming traffic. Grabbing his scruff again, Max pulled the red dog the rest of the way out of danger. The other two dogs stared in disbelief.

"You saved him," the yellow dog said in shock.

Carl regained his senses and looked up at Max in wonder.

"You did. You saved me."

Max shook his head from side to side, trying to free

his mouth from the awful taste of Carl's filthy fur. Then he sat down by the road to catch his breath. His heart beat so fast he could hear it pounding.

"Those headlights had me hypnotized," Carl said. "I couldn't move or think or anything."

"You know better than to look into the headlights, Carl," the yellow dog said.

"I know, I know, but you forget, and then there they are. Blam!"

All of the dogs turned to stare at Max again.

"What's your name, stranger?"

"The humans called me Max."

"The humans called me Tex," the yellow dog said. "Then they called me Bad Dog. Then they called me Dumb Dog. Then one day they drove by here, opened the car door, shoved me out, and drove away. Never saw them again. So much for humans."

The other two dogs nodded, their tongues hanging out in agreement.

Max had heard about people dumping dogs around here in the woods, but he'd never actually met a stray dog before—a dog with absolutely no humans to answer to at all.

"Hey, I know you," the daredevil dog said. "You live up at the top of the mountain."

Max sniffed at him hesitantly. Dusty? It was the neighbor's dog, Dusty. At least his tendency to run across the highway without thinking twice made some sense now. With Dusty recognizing him, it was pointless to deny where his house was. Max was just going to have to fess up with the whole truth.

"That's where I used to live," he admitted, "but I ran away a few hours ago. I followed a trail into the woods and realized that I could get away if I just kept going. So I did."

"Outstanding," Tex said. "Who needs humans anyhow?"

"My human's not so bad," Dusty whined.

"Fine, fine, Dusty. Your human is fine. But I notice you spend most of your time down here with us instead of up there at home."

Dusty stared at the ground sadly and then changed his mind about being upset. Jumping to his feet, tongue flapping, he hopped around Max three times.

"So now that you ran away, you are free to play, and play, and play!" he cheered.

Max supposed that he was right. He was free, and it was fantastic. Except for the not-eating part. That was no game. As if he could read Max's mind, Tex brought up the subject.

"We'd better look for some dinner before the sun comes up," he suggested.

"You haven't had dinner yet?" Max said. It had been hours and hours now since he had his. Dusty at least must have eaten at home before he ran down the hill to join his friends.

"Yeah," Dusty said. "I forgot about dinner. Too busy out running wild. AWHOOO!" he howled.

"AWHOOO!" the other wild dogs howled at the night sky in not very organized harmony. Then they turned to Max.

"Go on," Tex urged him. "You must have howled before."

Max considered it, and he couldn't think of a single time he had even considered howling. Barking, sure.

Howling? He had heard the glorious sounds the coyotes made. These dog sounds were an embarrassing substitute, but maybe he could pull one off.

He snuffled and hacked a bit to clear his throat.

"Oh, just do it!" Dusty barked.

"Awowowowowooo," Max managed to garble. It was not pretty. He dropped his head and wiped his front paw across his face.

"Well," Tex said. "That was interesting."

"Try again. Try again!" Dusty said, bouncing by the roadside.

"Don't worry about it," Carl said. "Think about the woods and the road and freedom. Let it run through your whole body. Then, just let it out."

Max closed his eyes. He thought about the moment when he decided to run. His legs twitched, remembering that decisive second he jumped the fence and headed into the unknown valley and the adventures that followed. Running away from a chomping mule. Following coyotes on a moonlit hunt. Hungry badgers. Saving Carl from a certain squishing on the highway. He was Max, the wild and free dog of the Ozark Mountains. The instinct of his ancestors coursed through his blood, and his hackles rose up in excitement. Throwing back his head, Max told the world that he was free. Wild and free!

"AWHOOO! AH AH AHWHOOO!" echoed from his mouth and off the mountains all around.

"Now, that's a howl," Carl said. The others nodded in appreciation.

"And now we eat," Tex said.

Max's body tingled all over from his first genuine wild howl, but he didn't see any food nearby. What was for dinner? Carl was already headed off down the highway.

"I thought I saw something along here earlier," he called back.

Something along the road? He doesn't mean... Max felt the hungry juices in his stomach gurgle. Munching on deer poop in the yard was mostly just for fun, and because it annoyed the Mama-lady so much. *Ewww, Max, NO!* But road kill?

"Found it!" Carl called back to his buddies.

They all trotted to where he was, with Max bringing

up the very reluctant rear. Yes, it was most definitely road kill, and an unmistakable stink rose up from it. Max knew that smell. Skunk.

I'm supposed to eat a dead skunk for dinner? He gagged a tiny bit at the very thought of it. *At least this time I can say I already ate. Not terribly hungry. Only ran away a few hours ago. As the new guy, it shouldn't be a big deal. I'd eat last anyhow.*

"Um, Max," Carl said. "You saved my life tonight. I can only think of one way to repay you."

The dogs all took a ceremonial step back from the skunk.

Oh, no. They want me to eat first!

Max knew what an honor this was. Tex most certainly should be the first to eat. It was clear he was the leader, but he had stepped back as well. To refuse would be offensive and downright rude. If he wanted to stay with these dogs at all, he was going to have to do it. He was going to have to take a serious bite of that smelly, nasty, squished up, dead skunk.

His nose twitched as he walked toward dinner. He sneezed quickly, trying to pretend he didn't. The trio of dogs stared and waited. Leaning down, Max closed his eyes, tried not to breathe, and opened his mouth to take a bite.

He should have done it. He should have taken a chunk, swallowed it quickly, and stepped back so the others could eat. But that's not what happened. It wasn't even close.

DINNER?

As much as Max wanted to be a good wild dog, he simply hadn't been free long enough. Food for Max still came in processed form—from a bag or a can. He had never really eaten raw meat, except a few scraps from the kitchen now and then. And skunk? Forget it. All his nose could process was that day years ago when he'd been sprayed. This wasn't food. He couldn't do it.

Instead of taking a bite, Max gagged. And not just a little gag. It was the kind of all out retching sound that he made after he ate too much grass in the yard and got it stuck in his throat.

Hhhaaaccckkk!

The dogs gasped in horror. Max hung his head in shame.

"I'm sorry. I really am."

"Not quite as wild and not quite as hungry as you thought you were," Tex said.

"I suppose not," Max admitted, his head hung low enough to touch the ground.

"You'll get there, my new friend. You'll get there," Tex assured him. Then he claimed the right of honor and grabbed a huge bite of the dead skunk. Each of the others followed in turn. Just watching them eat it made Max feel like he would hack again, but he kept it in check.

How hungry do you have to be to eat a dead skunk? Max wondered. Dusty couldn't be that hungry. He had food at home. Was there something Max was missing that would make road kill—smelly road kill—appealing? How desperate would he have to get for food? How desperate were Tex and Carl? Max wasn't too sure he enjoyed this side of wild and free.

Headlights shone along the road, coming down the mountain toward them. The group dashed back into the shadows of the tree line before the driver could spot them. Once the car passed, they all stood watching the red tail lights fade off into the distance.

"That was pretty much all of it anyhow," Carl mumbled, licking his jaws, which now smelled distinctly skunky.

"We might have better luck hunting frogs and snakes down by the stream," Tex suggested.

Snakes? Max gulped. *Don't snakes bite back?*

The Daddy-man was terrified of snakes. Once, not long after they moved to the house in the Ozark country, the whole family witnessed a giant, black rat snake crawling up the steps of the pavilion in the yard. The Mama-lady said he must be five or six feet long. She thought he was adorable and named him Clyde. The Daddy-man was not impressed or charmed. She made him promise not to hurt it because it was harmless. Max hoped none of them came face-to-face with it, ever. Fortunately, they never did.

They'd encountered smaller snakes over the years

that taught the Daddy-man to wear big boots and stomp his feet when they went walking in the woods. Max wondered if that's why the man did so much talking too. It was best to let snakes know you were coming. Most of them would get out of the way. Now Max was supposed to go hunting for one? For dinner? That hacking feeling started to tickle at the back of his throat again.

Tex led the way along a well-worn trail from the back of the abandoned house into the forest. They all trotted along confidently, and Max brought up the rear, hoping that those in the front would do the hunting. Eating a snake didn't sound quite as bad as the dead skunk, but it didn't sound very appealing either.

Soon afterward, they reached a clearing in the trees and a small stream, running down the side of the mountain and off to the King's River below. It sparkled and gurgled in the spring moonlight, and Max was suddenly sure of one thing. He was thirsty.

Without hesitation, the whole gang crouched at the edge of the stream and lapped up mouthful after mouthful of the fresh, cold water. Max was positive that no water had ever tasted so wonderful at any point in the history of the world. It made his whole body want to howl again.

When he had finally drunk all he could hold, Max sat down on the river bank and panted for air, his tongue lolling out of his mouth and dripping onto his white, spotted chest.

Probably should have done that a bit slower, he thought. A huge belch vibrated up from his stomach.

Brrraaach.

"Well done!" Tex laughed.

Max's stomach made a loud gurgling noise in response.

"Now, let's get us some more chow," Carl said.

He trotted around the edge of the spring until he spotted his first victim. A large frog was resting on a rock on the far side of the stream. Carl froze. Then he hunkered down, keeping his eyes on the frog. Hearing the scrabbling in the rocks nearby, the frog opened one eye. He regarded the dog, but he didn't move. Max watched in fascination.

Catching a frog was actually something Max had

tried before. Many times. They were slippery little creatures and always managed to jump away at the last second, when you were sure you had them, and your jaws would clamp shut on nothing but air. Or on your own tongue. Max had done that a time or two as well. Carl began to waggle his rear end, preparing for the attack.

"Back off," the frog croaked.

"Ah, little froggy," Carl mumbled, "you will be my dinner."

"Doubt it," the frog croaked.

Max sensed that this wasn't the first time this particular frog had dealt with a dog.

Carl took his waggle into high gear, raising his swaying bottom up off the ground. Then he leapt. So did the frog. Carl landed on the empty rock and then fell into the water, and the frog splashed down easily into the stream, allowing it to carry him out of reach. Tex just laughed.

"You'll never get 'em if they know you're coming," he said.

"Aw, I was mostly getting warmed up," Carl laughed,

shaking off his long, red fur as he climbed out of the water on the other side of the stream.

"Get 'em to hop, then you snatch them out of the air, like this."

Tex took off along the bank of the stream, scattering frogs left and right, snapping at them as they fled. Carl started the same rousting on his side of the river too. Dusty joined in, but Max could tell he was mostly playing. He could have dinner anytime he wanted back at his house. Some of the fleeing frogs started to head in Max's direction. Yes, he was hungry enough to try for a frog.

The next hour was spent chasing the hopping creatures and splashing in the stream—and sometimes even catching a frog. Tex got several. Carl got a couple. So did Dusty. Max caught one, but once he had it in his mouth he discovered that it tasted disgusting and was covered in a nasty slime.

He dropped the frog on the ground in front of him. For a minute the creature looked stunned and didn't move. Maybe it was hoping the dog couldn't see it in the semi-dark. Max looked up to see if the other dogs had noticed him spit the frog out, but they were too busy on their own hunts. When he looked back down, the frog was gone.

He was wrong. He was not hungry enough to eat a frog. Not just yet.

Farther downstream, Tex growled a deep rumble in his throat that stopped the other dogs in their tracks. It took a second for Max's eyes to adjust to the darker part of the forest where Tex was standing. The yellow dog had his feet firmly planted in a defensive position and was staring intently at the ground, ears on full alert, but Max couldn't see what he was looking at.

Then he heard it. They all heard it. Max's fur stood on end.

"Back off," the frog croaked.

12

SAVED BY THE BARK

atch out, Tex," Carl called from his spot across the stream. Max wasn't sure what to do or say to help the yellow dog. The four of them were smack-dab in the middle of one of the Daddy-man's worst fears. Tex snarled again, and the creature on the ground answered him as only it could.

Ssststststststs. It was a warning and a threat at the same time.

"This ain't my first rattler," Tex said through bared teeth. "Maybe he could make a nice dessert."

Ssststststststs. The snake's tail vibrated in the leaves again in warning. *Do not mess with me, or I will mess with you.*

"Whoa, whoa, whoa," Dusty barked. "Just back away now, Tex. It ain't worth it."

Ssststststststs.

From somewhere deep in Max's herding, protecting instinct, information he had never had reason to consider swirled in his brain. He knew exactly what to do.

"We can distract him," he said.

He now had the full attention of Dusty and Carl. Tex didn't flinch or drop his gaze from the furious snake.

"If the snake is distracted for even a minute, you can run and not get bitten."

"How's that snake know I'm not the one who's gonna bite him?" Tex snarled.

"Don't be stupid," Carl said. "Rattlers ain't nothing to be messed with. The woods are full of snakes we can have for dessert if we want. This one just ain't worth it."

"He's right, Tex," Max said. "You may be quick, but that snake is going to defend himself to the bitter end. One bite is all it will take out here with no humans to help."

"I don't need no dumb humans," Tex growled, leaning his head slightly toward the snake.

Sssststststststs.

The rattling grew louder as the snake lifted the tip of his tail out of the leaves, showing it to Tex. Max could see the snake's tongue flicking in and out of his mouth, picking the best spot for a clean strike with fangs that were certainly at the ready.

"Okay, I believe you. We don't need any humans, but you really don't need rattlesnake for dessert," Max said. "Carl, when I say GO, you run and bark at the snake from the far side. I'll run at him from this side. Tex, all you need to do is back up. Carl and I will scare him enough that he may strike at us, so don't get too close, Carl."

"I hear ya," Carl said. "We'll just shake him up a bit so he's distracted, and Tex can get away bite-free."

"Yes, that's it exactly."

"What do ya want me to do?" Dusty chimed in.

"Watch behind Tex as he runs," Max said. "If the snake is angry enough to chase him, you can make it think twice by just barking loudly and scaring it away."

Ssststststststs.

"He sounds pretty angry," Dusty said.

"I know, so let's get this moving fast. Are you ready, Tex?"

"Fine. But I don't really need saving. I can take him."

"No man, don't do it," Carl begged. "I can't watch ya get bit!"

"All right," Tex relented. "Max, when you say GO, I'll run."

Ssststststststs.

Ssststststststs.

SSSTSTSTSTSTSTSTS.

The snake seemed to sense that some plan was afoot. He raised his head up out of the leaves, tongue flicking faster and faster.

"Okay," Max said. "On the count of three."

The other dogs moved into position—eyes bright, hackles up, and ready.

"One. Two. Three. GO!"

Max ran toward Tex and the snake from his side, barking like a wild demon. Carl ran at them from the other, snapping at the air and yapping as loud as he could. The snake hissed and spit, head swaying and eyes glinting in the moonlight, not sure which side to defend. That was enough for Tex to break free and run. Dusty was ready, but the snake didn't give chase. With so many dogs barking and running at it, the snake made a hasty retreat into the leaves and undergrowth behind it.

"Woo Hoo! It worked," Carl cheered.

Max sat down where he was, panting and tingling from the adrenaline rush. Wild and free! He had saved his new friend from a nasty death at the hands of a venomous snake. Fantastic! But then his blood slowed and his head cleared.

Did I just run at a snake? he wondered. *What if it had decided to jump at me instead?* Max had heard the Daddy-man explain to his daughters how a doctor could give you a shot if a snake bit you, but what if there was no doctor or vet to help out?

Max watched as the dog pack leapt and splashed around in the stream and celebrated their victory, but the tame side of Max could only sit and think about how it might have all turned out very differently. If Tex had been bitten, that could have been the end of Tex.

Wild and free came with big risks. And for Max it still came with an empty stomach. His belly grumbled in agreement.

Exhausted, the other three dogs lumbered over to where Max sat. They all collapsed around him.

"You the man, Max!" Carl gasped. "I thought he was a goner for sure."

"I don't know where it came from," Max admitted. "It was like a movie played in my head about exactly how to trick that snake."

"Instinct, my man," Carl said. "That's pure instinct. Stuff tucked way down in our minds that we don't need much in the human world."

"Too bad we couldn't have that snake for dessert,"

Dusty huffed. "Snake meat is dee-lish-ious." His tongue hung out of his mouth, and a little string of drool dripped off. "My human gets one every now and then. Fries it up over the campfire. Mmm, mmm."

Max tried to imagine his Daddy-man catching and eating a rattlesnake. No. That would never happen. They might live in the country, but his humans were still city folks when it came to things like that.

"I think we can all just be grateful that we got out of that with our tails in one piece," Tex said. "Crickets are an easier and safer dessert. Much less chance of getting bit."

Crickets? Max had eaten his share of crickets and June bugs back in Houston when he was young and silly. On evening walks, Max could grab them right out of the air. The Daddy-man used to tease him that they were his chips and Cheetos. *Crunch. Crunch.* It was fun to catch the flittery things, but he wouldn't want to have to survive on them. They were mostly crunch and not much else.

"Do you get tired of having to hunt for your food all the time?" Max asked. "With only frogs and crickets and some occasional road kill, it seems like it would take a lot of work just to fill your stomach."

The other three dogs looked at each other, exchanging glances that Max couldn't quite interpret.

"Hunting frogs is a blast!" Dusty barked.

"Well," Tex said, "Dusty here isn't really the best example. He gets dinner from his human and table scraps and all kinds of other nonsense along the way. Having dinner with us is just for fun." Dusty looked at the ground, a bit ashamed. "Carl and I don't have much choice. We don't have humans to care for us, so we make the best of it."

Carl shook his head, slobber flying, and then snorted.

"I've had a few masters along the way. Ain't never found humans to be that reliable when it comes to caring for dogs. Best to take care of your own hide."

Max wasn't sure how to respond to that. The Daddy-man never let him go hungry. He always had plenty of food and water and care. Maybe Carl just hadn't met the right human yet.

"Getting dinner handed to me in a metal bowl starts to sound better and better as the years go by,"

Tex admitted. "I'm getting slower and the frogs seem to get faster."

Looking at Tex and Carl, bedraggled from their romp in the stream and ribs showing from never quite having enough to eat, Max had a brilliant idea.

"You know, there's a farm up the hill where dogs like you could find a good meal and maybe even a job."

Tex raised one eyebrow, doubting such a place existed.

"It's off the highway a bit, so you'll have to walk up the long driveway, but there are chickens to be guarded and probably lots of other things that need doing that I didn't see in the little while that I was there."

"Chickens make a good dinner," Carl said, drooling again.

"No, No," Max said. "There's an old dog there guarding them, and he means business. He'll make a fuss and the man will come out with a gun. Attacking the farm would only get you one meal, at best. It might even get you shot. But if you slunk in there and looked lost and sad, I bet you could find a home."

The pair of stray dogs stared at the ground for several minutes, considering this option. Carl's ears and eyebrows seemed to have a mind of their own, raising and lowering as his mind spun with the possibilities.

"Would you want a home with a human bossing you around?" Dusty asked, stunned.

Tex dragged his front claws through the rocky ground in front of him. Carl looked from Tex to Dusty to Max, waiting for his friend to answer.

"Well now," Tex said, "it's not the worst idea I've heard all day."

Dusty sneezed and shook his head in dismay. Tex, the wild and rebellious feral dog with no use for humans, was his hero. He wasn't sure what to do with this willing-to-be-tame creature in front of him, but Max understood.

"What about all that stuff about not needing humans?" Dusty whined.

"Well, I may have been showing off a bit there," Tex admitted. "We aren't coyotes or wolves, Dusty. Dogs have been conditioned and bred and trained to live with humans over hundreds of years. We still have a little wild in our blood, but mostly our instinct is to be with a human and care for a home. All dogs, given the choice of a kind master, would rather be owned than free. My humans never gave me that choice."

"From what I sensed from Odin and Thor at the farmhouse, their owner is good and kind and takes care of them. They were the most loyal dogs I've ever met."

Tex sighed deeply and lifted his head high. Carl nodded in agreement.

"Wild is good, but a safe home is always better for a dog. So maybe you could point the way to that farmhouse, Max."

*The snake seemed to sense that some plan
was afoot. He raised his head up out of the
leaves, tongue flicking faster and faster.*

13

DANGER LURKS

After Max had explained how to find Odin and Thor's solar-roof farmhouse, the stray dogs realized they knew exactly where to go. The smell of chickens had been tempting more than once, but the threat of humans and other dogs had kept them from trying.

"Odin is the guard dog in charge," Max warned them. "Be sure he knows you've come for a home, not the chickens. There's a little dog named Thor there too who will threaten to kill you. Don't worry too much about him. He's all bark."

"Did you see the owner?" Carl asked.

"Yes, he was an old man, but he used Good Dog freely. He seemed kind."

"A kind human," Tex pondered. "That would be something to meet."

"My humans were kind enough, I guess," Max said. "They just never wanted me to be free."

"Free ain't all that it might seem," Carl snorted. "We survived the winter, but it wasn't pretty. I thought those coyotes might come hunting for us when the food got scarce. I'd rather not end my days as coyote chow."

Max thought about his time with the coyotes and was grateful he hadn't met them in the dead of a cold winter with little food. Maybe he would run into Winema and Kaliska and Yutu again in a few months. Would they be so kind? Max shook his head to scatter the scary images of that future meeting. Winter was too far away to worry about now.

It was nearing dawn. Dusty decided to head home back up the highway so he knew he wouldn't get lost. He had breakfast and a warm bed already waiting for him.

"Stay on the shoulder of the road, Dusty, off the concrete," Tex warned him. "Pay attention to where you're going."

Dusty barked his agreement and trotted in a zigzag path back to the road. Tex and Carl exchanged worried glances, and Max sensed heavy tension in the air.

"Dusty is not the smartest of dogs," Tex explained. "He's fun to hang out with, but you never know if he's gonna walk right in front of a semi-truck on the road because he forgot the highway was there."

"Maybe he will stick closer to home if we are not around to play with anymore," Carl said.

"He lives across the highway from my old house," Max said. "He runs right out into the road all the time. My human gets very upset and takes him back home. He says Dusty won't live to be an old dog if he doesn't get some sense in his head."

"We can only hope his own human keeps better tabs on him in the future," Tex said, but none of them really thought that it was likely.

Tex snorted and trotted over to the stream for one

last drink of water. Carl and Max followed. Frogs jumped out of their way, but none of the dogs were interested in frog hunting any more that night. After another belly full of that cold, clean water, Tex took up the lead along the stream heading uphill to where the farmhouse and a good human waited for him. Carl and Max followed, though Max wasn't sure what he would do when they got there.

The trees were thinner around the stream, so it made for an excellent travel path. The bright moonlight flooded down, and they could see each rock and tree root that waited to trip them up. Carl wandered into the creek every now and then, just to splash in the water, as they worked their way upstream.

Carl had just jumped back onto the bank and sprayed cold water everywhere with a massive head-to-toe shake when the trio heard a large cracking noise from the woods. *Kerrrwak!* All three froze in place. It sounded like a giant tree limb had been snapped clean in two. Could it be the coyotes?

Ears on full alert, Max heard more snapping and shuffling, along with a low grumbling that didn't come from any creature he had ever met before.

A deep whine reverberated from Tex, and Carl lowered his head until it almost touched the ground.

"Should we run or hide?" Carl asked.

"I don't think he's seen us yet," Tex whispered, a whine still tinging every word. "But I can't smell him, so we must be downwind. He's bound to catch our scent any second."

"What is it?" Max said.

"A bear. And it sounds like a big one."

Max had never come close to encountering a bear, but he had seen them on TV shows. Words like "attack" and "maul" flashed through his memory. Nothing about being face-to-face with a big bear in the dark forest was good.

"We've been coming here for a few months," Tex said. "He must have still been asleep, hibernating somewhere. A groggy spring bear is a problem."

As the dogs debated what to do, the rustlings stopped. They heard the beast sniffing at the air. He had discovered them. A low growl vibrated in the dark trees.

Hrrrmmmrrrmmmrrrmmm.

"Maybe he's not hungry," Max hoped.

"Hungry's got nothing to do with it," Tex growled. "This must be his turf. Bears will defend their territory…" He glanced at the other two, the whites of his eyes showing. "They defend it to the death."

With a mighty crash, the bear's head burst out of the forest, and the dogs found themselves staring straight at a brown bear that stood at least a head taller than any of them. He sniffed the air again, and then he curled his lips to reveal long, fearsome fangs.

"Water mine!" the bear growled.

Hiding was no longer an option, so the dogs instinctively did what their ancestors had done for generations when confronted with an angry opponent without hope of winning the standoff.

They ran.

RUN FOR YOUR LIVES

I f you are human, running from a bear is a terrible idea. But if you are a dog who is fleet-footed and swift and can see in the dark woods, you have a chance of outrunning him. So they ran.

The dogs didn't look back to see if he was following. They just ran flat out along the riverbank with Max in the lead.

"Head for the farmhouse!" Tex hollered up to him. "The man has a gun. If the bear's chasing us, human scent should stop him.

The trees grew closer together the farther upstream

they ran, and it was harder and harder to see. Max worried more about his next steps than he did about where the other two dogs were. The flash of the bear's teeth and the uncertainty and fear that he could be not far behind was enough to keep him running, even if it was mostly blindly.

His tongue flapped out of the side of his mouth, and he gasped for air, but he ran. Before long, he realized that he couldn't hear Tex and Carl behind him anymore. *Did the bear get them?* No, he would have heard that. He shuddered at the thought.

Max slowed to a trot and listened for his new friends. Nothing. Stopping completely, he tuned in to the sounds of the forest around him. An owl in a tree. The stream gurgling. But there was no other movement.

The farmhouse. Max had forgotten that he was supposed to run to the farmhouse. Tex and Carl had known the way. They must have turned off into the woods and headed for the solar house, not realizing that Max was still running up ahead. His black fur would have been nearly invisible to them racing along behind him.

Looking around the woods, Max had no idea how to get to the farmhouse from there. He had found it from the driveway along the freeway. In this part of the woods it was trees, trees, everywhere trees. He couldn't smell the chickens. No sign of Tex or Carl. Most importantly, he couldn't hear or smell the bear. They had been running uphill for a good while. It must have quit chasing them.

So, once again, Max found himself all alone in the dark forest. Wild and free, but all alone. It had been fun to be a part of a pack, even if only for a short while. It felt right. Dogs are pack animals. They are not designed to live alone. He hoped Tex and Carl had found the solar roof farmhouse and that the human would take them in. Maybe he would visit them if he ever found the highway again.

Taking a quick drink from the stream, Max worked on catching his breath. The only sound around him was the stream and his own panting. It was decision time again. Never in his whole life had he made as many choices as he had made on this one wild night.

He could get to the highway by following the stream back down the mountain, but a bear blocked his path.

Nope. He didn't want to go that way.

He could head off into the part of the woods that looked like it sloped down into the valley, but that was probably where the mule and his chomping teeth were waiting. Nope. He didn't want to go that way either.

The stream was no longer leading directly uphill, so he could follow it and see where it took him. At least he would have a landmark and always know exactly where he was. *Follow the stream* was the answer, so he started off at a slow walk, letting his heart rate get back to normal.

Alone with his thoughts, Max felt a tug at his heart. The sun would be up soon. He could feel the air changing around him. Back at his house, the cats would wake up first. If he had been home, they would wander past his kennel to their food bowl. Maybe they would try to smell his toes or bat at his tail through the bars.

Silly cats, he thought, despite his best efforts to remember them as annoying.

It was a school day, so the family would wake up

early to alarm clocks that buzzed without mercy. Daddy would set him free from the kennel and give him a big bowl of breakfast. His stomach complained.

No one will be bringing me breakfast today, he thought.

If he was at home, Daddy would let him run and play in the yard for a while after breakfast to check out all the morning smells. What animals had wandered through his yard that night? Centuries of instinct made him feel guilty for not knowing what was happening at his house. That house, those people, even those cats, were his responsibility. His duty. They were his pack.

Max stopped to consider that. Did he need other dogs in order to have a pack, or was it just the lives that were tied to his? What were they all going to do without him? A feeling deep in his bones niggled and tickled and scratched at his heart. What was it that he was feeling? It was something different from the wild and free he'd experienced so far that night.

Is this what lonely feels like? he wondered.

In his whole life, Max had never had a chance to

feel lonely. Even at the shelter before he was adopted, other dogs and humans were always around. *Wild and free comes at a price,* Tex had said. Maybe lonely was part of that price. Max didn't know much, but he knew this wasn't part of his dream to be wild and free. It was as stinky as a dead skunk. A little whine slipped out. He was all alone and hungry in the dark woods at night. It was not as much fun as he had expected it to be.

Then he noticed something at the edge of the trees next to him. The wooden fence! He gave it a quick sniff. Max suddenly knew exactly where he was. This was his fence. It separated his property from the cattle fields below where the crabby mule waited to nip at unsuspecting dogs. Jumping through the middle of the logs, Max found his feet were now back on his own land and on a trail that he knew as well as the spots on his belly. Still, he wasn't sure what to do.

The whole night had been such a jumble of strange adventures. Coyotes and chickens and a mule. Old Dog Odin and Tiny Thor with his chant of *Kill, Kill.* Risking his hide with a snake and even a bear. What could ever begin to compare to this night of wild and free life?

Climbing the mountain back to his warm, safe house seemed like the wise thing to do, but it would be a major letdown as well. Instead, Max trotted down the path and into the trees where he knew of a special place he could rest and think. Daddy loved to go there and took Max with him most of the time.

"Let's go check the cave," Daddy would say. *Cave.* Max knew that word as clearly as he knew the word *dinner.* Going to check out the cave meant that they would head off into the forest together. They would be man and dog alone in the woods. Sometimes Daddy would bring his gun. "Just in case," he would say, but he never had to fire it. All those creatures living in the forest scurried out of the way of a man and his faithful dog.

Max wasn't feeling very faithful at that moment. With a heavy heart, he turned from the fence line and climbed up the slope leading to the little cave on his property. It wasn't very big, but it provided a safe view of the valley all around.

Daddy had shown him the black char marks on the roof of the cave. They were proof that fires had been built there, maybe from where Native Americans might have sought a safe place to spend the night. Nothing could sneak up on you when you were inside the cave facing out. Max sat in the opening and marveled at the view around him. He had never experienced it in the moonlight before.

From this vantage point, he could see the mule's valley and brown smudges scattered around on the ground that must be the sleeping cows. He scanned the surrounding mountains and spotted a light here and there that must be from a hidden house. The Ozarks were sleeping and quiet and peaceful, not quite ready to face the dawn of a new day.

Grrruuummmrrrr.

Something behind Max grumbled. *Oh no.* Something was in the cave with him.

Ears and hackles immediately alert, Max tested the air for what might be there in the dark. Too terrified to turn around, he couldn't smell anything, but he heard the scraping of rock and a shuffling sound. After the longest night of his life, a night filled with dangers and hunger and more walking than he normally did in a month, Max couldn't take any more.

That unknown creature behind him in what he thought was the safest spot in the world was the last straw. There was no Daddy with a gun to protect him. Without a second thought, Max jumped from the entrance of the cave and ran. Crashing through overgrown bushes and shrubs, leaping over low hanging limbs, crunching violently through the leaves, Max ran home.

15

HOME SWEET HOME

Max didn't need his nose to find the way. From the cave, all he needed to do was go up and up and up. Through the trees, rocks slipping under his feet, he climbed and climbed and climbed until he finally stepped out into the clearing at the top of the mountain. His house still stood there, like it had been waiting patiently for him to return.

Panting for air to catch his breath, Max plopped down in his own yard. The rush of freedom had worn off, and all Max felt was exhausted. Being wild was exhausting. Being free was lonely and terrifying. All he wanted now was to eat and rest and be safe. Ambling around to the front of the house, Max dragged his tired body up the front steps and onto the deck. The lights were still off inside the house, but Max knew that nothing wild would come onto his porch. They wouldn't dare.

Wearily, Max climbed up onto one of the big, red deck chairs that Daddy liked to use for reading and contemplating life. Max looked out over the miles and miles of mountains around him. Sitting there, watching the sun rise, Max wondered if Mama and Daddy were as grateful for this safe, warm home as he was right at that moment. He was tempted to curl up and go to sleep. Every bone and muscle in his body wanted nothing more than sleep and food, but he forced himself to stay awake. If Daddy came looking for him, he wanted to be alert and ready to respond.

The sun was still glowing red and orange in the sky when Max heard the familiar creaking of the old wood floors of the living room. The latch on the door behind him clicked, and there was Daddy, standing in the doorway in his pajamas.

"Well, what do you know?" he said, running his fingers through his hair sleepily. "After all that fuss, here you are just having a morning cup of coffee on the porch."

Max had no interest in coffee, but he had never been so grateful to see a human being in his entire life. Not even the day that Mama selected him out of all the other dogs at the shelter. Back then, he really didn't understand what it meant to be hungry and lost. Today, he did. Now he just wanted back into his house with his family. His pack. He wanted to herd his cats around and make sure he knew where each and every human was every second of every day until his muzzle was as gray as Odin's. All of that leapt through his heart in one beat, but what came out of his mouth was one long, exhausted, raspy whine.

Max stumbled off the porch chair and walked slowly past Daddy into the house, head hung low. He knew what was coming.

Bad Dog.

He deserved it. He would take the scolding that he knew he had coming. He had run away instead of coming back when Daddy called. *Bad, Bad Dog.*

But Daddy didn't say it.

"It's nice to have you back home again," was all he said as Max staggered by. "Mama was very worried."

Max stopped and snuffled in the smells of home— all the creatures and furniture and walls and floors that were his responsibility to protect. Pride swelled in his chest. He understood what Odin had tried to explain. Living with the humans and protecting them is a solemn duty. It must never be forsaken or taken lightly. Max knew he would never take it for granted again.

"Where'd your collar go?" Daddy asked, ruffling the thick fur around his neck. "Guess we will have to get you a new one. At least you still had your microchip. Any vet or shelter worth its salt would have scanned you and found that. You'd have made it home one way or another."

A microchip? Max wasn't sure what a microchip was, but it made his heart warm to know that he had one. Daddy had made sure that his dog would always find his way back to them. He was a marked dog. There was no way around it.

The little white cat sauntered up to him and touched noses.

"Where have you been?" she asked. "Daddy was out looking for you for hours. You made him very sad. Mama too."

"I was lost," he said. "I hope it never happens again."

"Me too," the white cat agreed and rubbed her body around and around on his tired legs, stopping to bat at his slowly wagging tail. "Who would we have to boss us around if our Big Black Beast were gone? We would miss you."

Max swished his tail on purpose twice more so the cat would have something to chase.

"I bet you have some stories to tell about last night," Daddy joked. "What kind of trouble can a dog get into in these mountains alone at night?"

You have no idea, Max thought, eyeing his fluffy pillow across the room.

"How about some breakfast before you catch up on your sleep?"

Max heard his tummy grumble and looked up at Daddy.

Yes, breakfast would be fantastic.

Following Daddy to his big, metal bowl, Max ambled along on sore paw pads. The rocky Ozark ground had not been kind to them. The wood floors of the house that used to seem so hard felt soft as feathers under them now. Daddy watched as Max approached slowly.

"No dance for your breakfast today?"

Max just sat down with a grunt in front of his bowl. *No. No dance.* He was happy he had the energy to make it across the room to the food dish. Dancing would have to wait.

Daddy scooped up some food nuggets, and they plunked down into the big, metal bowl like delightful music. Max started to eat, but Daddy came back with another scoop. Max never got two scoops for breakfast. He gazed up into Daddy's face.

"I'll bet you're extra hungry this morning," he said gently.

Too hungry and too tired to answer, Max simply crunched away on what was surely the most delicious meal in the whole universe.

"Good boy, Max," Daddy said, patting his shoulders. "Good Dog."

Yes, Max thought. *Only Good Dog from now on.*

A soft bed and a crunchy bone.
Home Sweet Home.

EPILOGUE

Max leapt over tree branches and ducked under low hung limbs as he raced through the forest, hot on the trail of a new amazing smell. He was wild and free! Nothing could stop him! As he crashed into a clearing at the bottom of the mountain, the ornery mule met him face-to-face.

"Get out of my field, you mangy mutt!" he brayed.

"Make me!" Max barked back, snapping his fierce jaws at the snout of that annoying, bossy mule.

"Run!" the mule yelled to the cows resting in the

grass nearby. "Run for your lives! This one's crazy!"

Every cow in the pasture staggered to her feet, the mule running and braying and waking each of them up.

"There's no escaping him!" the mule hollered, heehawing loud enough to wake every herd animal for miles around. "Flee! Save the babies! Run!"

"Max?" Mama whispered. "Max, are you okay?"

Opening one eye, Max woke to find himself sprawled out on his fluffy pillow in the corner of the living room. Well, sort of on his pillow. He'd managed to work his way halfway off so his head and shoulder were now on the floor.

"That must have been some dream," Mama chuckled. "You run in your sleep all the time, but sleep barking is very impressive."

Max wasn't sure if he was sadder to wake up from the dream or happier to be safe at home. Having animals run in fear of him was exciting, but after his real night of wild and free, he now knew the whole picture. Dreaming about it was better than living it.

But he could still dream about it whenever he

wanted.

Max closed his eyes, and soon he was racing through the woods again, hot on the trail.

The End

Max, surveying the valley from his mountaintop.

AUTHOR'S NOTE:

I hope you enjoyed Max's story. This companion book to my Cats in the Mirror series came from the frequent requests for a "dog book." Not everyone is a cat fan. I understand that. And many people who would stop at my booths to appreciate the book covers were sad when there was not a book for them. I hope this fits the need. Max himself was rarely more than a few feet away while I was writing it, so it has had his direct supervision—as do most things in our home.

Max, right under my
feet, as always.

Max came to join our family in 2006, after our move to Houston, Texas. He was already a year old and had been living in a no-kill shelter and foster homes since he was a puppy. We had promised our girls a dog when we got a fenced yard. A black-and-white one was what we had in mind because it matched our cats. My husband, Scott, was hoping for a male dog.

I snuck off to the shelter one day to look for a candidate and surprise them. After wandering through the selections for a while without finding that one who was just right, Max came bursting back into the room, waggling from head to toe. He had been outside. *Oh, there he is,* I thought. I knew he was our dog from that moment on.

Those first few weeks were trying, to say the least. Max is super smart with great Border Collie instincts, but he lacked discipline and didn't know how to channel his skills or energy. After a few training classes, Max and I figured each other out. I learned how to direct him and communicate in a way he understood, and he learned that I was the alpha dog. He has been a wonderful and loved member of our family ever since.

Max actually did run away for an entire night in the Ozark Mountains, and we found him sitting on the porch chair waiting for us in the morning. Whether he got lost on a trail, or whether he simply decided to have a wild night like in this book, we will never know. He's never shared his motives or his experiences with me. I'd love to say that was the last time that Max ended up in the woods following a scent, but it most certainly was not. There are some odors that he just must investigate, no matter how far afield it takes him.

The stories that Max remembers in the book are based on true events. He was sprayed by a skunk while the family was geocaching one night. (If you have never heard of geocaching, you can find out more about that activity at geocaching.com.) We do have a cave that he and Daddy like to visit, and he did run away from me in our Houston neighborhood to the great delight of some Mexican landscapers. You can even find a video of his "dinner dance" at my YouTube channel (you can find the link in the sidebar at my website, www.megdendler.com).

If you are a reader of the Cats in the Mirror books, you should recognize Max as The Big Black Beast from those books. You may have also caught the reference to a group of feral cats in the woods that Odin warns Max to avoid. Those would be the rebel alien cats sent to Earth at the end of *Miss Fatty Cat's Revenge* as a part of Operation Ozark Occupation. And, of course, the small white cat that Max talks to at the end of the book is Kimba.

The little cheetah-like cat Max mentions is our Brown Spotted Tabby, Cheetara, who is new to our family. She and Max have become best buddies and have their own special games (you can find videos of them playing at my YouTube site as well). She has not been introduced in the Cats in the Mirror series yet, but I already have plans for her in *Kimba's Christmas*.

I always select names for my characters with great care. For the coyotes, I thought I would go with some Native American words. The name Winema means chief, which seemed logical for the leader of the pack. Kaliska is a Miwok name that means "coyote chasing deer," and Yutu is Miwok meaning "coyote out hunting." (www.showwowl.com) Cheyenne is in honor of the lone coyote at Turpentine Creek Wildlife Refuge (where Kimba is sent in *Miss Fatty Cat's Revenge* and I am a real-life docent).

When deciding on the best sarcastic name for the tiny killer dog, I could just imagine someone naming a dog like that Thor. Going with Odin for the wise, old guard dog was an easy step from that. Dusty is loosely based on a dog that used to live across the road from us. Carl seemed like an odd, goofy name for a dog, and Tex fit the alpha, yellow lab image I have of that poor, long-suffering stray.

As far as Max pulling Carl from the road, there are many videos on YouTube of one dog saving or pulling another to safety on roads. Some of them are difficult to watch, so I'm not sharing any links, but it's a real thing. That instinct to protect a pack member is strong.

Yes, dogs can see in the dark in light that is five times dimmer than humans, but not quite as well as cats. Dogs' eyes have a mirror-like membrane called a *tapetum lucidum* that allows light to rebound off the retina, letting it take in more light. Cats, birds, fish, and nocturnal hunters have the same type of eye system. So Max would have been able to see pretty well in the woods under the full moon. And if you saw him from a distance, his eyes would have had that same "eyeshine" that always looks so creepy in the dark.

After some research on badgers, I must admit that I am pretty impressed with them. Various species of badgers live all over the world, and they are fierce enough to protect their young from wild dogs, coyotes, and even bears. Badgers do live in Northwest Arkansas, where Max ran wild, but they are very rare. Thor and Odin would probably never have smelled one before. I had to add the part about the coyotes giving the badger hunting tips because those two creatures hunting in partnership has actually been documented. That's amazing! (Cahalane, VH

(1950). "Badger-coyote 'partnerships.'" Journal of Mammalogy 31: 354–355.)

As always, many thanks go out to my husband, Scott, for reading and reviewing and encouraging me to get this book done. He is Daddy in this book, and Max loves every bit of attention he can get from him. I am Mama, and I'm the boss, but Daddy is his buddy. They have spent many hours exploring our property and the cave together.

Thank you to my daughter Callista for using her stellar artistic talents to draw all of the illustrations in the book. Your art career has begun!

I should also express appreciation for my editor, Kathy Lapeyre (http://www.indiepublications.com), and my outstanding cover designer, Leslie Hollinger Vernon (http://lvdesignhouse.com). We have many books ahead of us too.

Thanks also to my beta readers: Justin Bush (my great-nephew), my daughters (whom readers know as Mindy and Leia), and my mom. And, of course, thanks to you too, Max.

Good Dog.

Don't miss Meg's other dog adventure book!

Dottie's Daring Day

BEST SELLING AUTHOR

By Meg Welch Dendler

Also by Meg Welch Dendler

Cats in the Mirror series

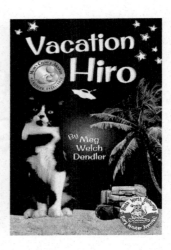

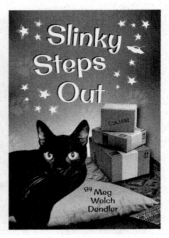

ABOUT THE AUTHOR

Meg Welch Dendler is a best-selling, award-winning author and a former teacher who celebrated publishing her first book, *Why Kimba Saved The World,* on February 23, 2013. This story is based on her true-life crazy cat and the other cats in her home... and the idea that they are all really part of an alien race from another planet. In October of 2013, *Why Kimba Saved The World* was honored with a Bronze Moonbeam Children's Book Award as "Best First Book — Chapter Book."

Both *Why Kimba Saved The World* and the sequel, *Vacation Hiro*, were honored with Silver Mom's Choice Awards for excellence in products for children in February of 2014. Books 1 and 2 are also "Story Monster Approved."

For over 10 years, Meg worked as a freelance writer, including a year as a columnist for www.religionandspirituality.com, where she wrote movie commentaries and interviews. She has had over 100 articles published in newspapers, magazines, and on websites, and has had the chance to interview Sylvester Stallone, Dwayne "The Rock" Johnson, Kirk Douglas, as well as Ioan Gruffudd and the Archbishop of Cape Town. She is a huge movie fan and prefers watching a new movie over most of what is on television.

An avid supporter of Character Education, Meg served as a teacher and community trainer for CHARACTER COUNTS! and has spoken about the integration of literature in character education programs at MiAEYC conferences and for the Arkansas Association of School Librarians.

Meg is a proud member of the Society of Children's Book Writers and Illustrators (SCBWI) and the Ozark

Writer's League (OWL).

A Texas native, Meg grew up in the Midwest area of Champaign-Urbana, Illinois, and then moved to the Metro Detroit suburbs when she was 13. She earned her undergraduate degree in Public Relations from Eastern Michigan University and returned to school there to earn her teaching certification and Master's Degree in Early Childhood Education.

After decades in Michigan, she and her family moved to Houston, Texas, in 2005. Making a total life and career change, in 2012 they bought seven acres of Ozark Mountain paradise, opened a rental guest house business, and focused on allowing Meg time to write and publish.

Trained and experienced as a public speaker and a certified teacher in Arkansas, Meg would love to visit your school or bookstore to share her books, have a read-aloud session, and promote reading and literacy for elementary school children.

You can follow Meg's blog and other social media links at her website: megdendler.com.

CPSIA information can be obtained
at www.ICGtesting.com
Printed in the USA
LVOW13s2326080118
562347LV00010B/119/P